BATTLE BUGS

THE LIZARD WAR

JACK PATTON

With special thanks to Tracey Turner

Scholastic Children's Books
An imprint of Scholastic Ltd
Euston House, 24 Eversholt Street, London, NW1 1DB, UK
Registered office: Westfield Road, Southam, Warwickshire, CV47 0RA
SCHOLASTIC and associated logos are trademarks and/or
registered trademarks of Scholastic Inc.

First Published in the US by Scholastic Inc, 2015
First published in the UK by Scholastic Ltd, 2015

Text copyright © Hot House Fiction, 2015
Cover and interior illustration art copyright © Mike Love, 2015
Paper Engineering copyright © Glen Coleman, 2015

ISBN 978 1407 15216 5

A CIP catalogue record for this book
is available from the British Library.

Printed by CPI Group (UK) Ltd, Croydon, CR0 4YY
Papers used by Scholastic Children's Books are made
from wood grown in sustainable forests.

1 3 5 7 9 10 8 6 4 2

www.scholastic.co.uk

BB

AN OLD BOOK

Max Darwin held his breath. Two fearsome barbed pincers appeared over the top of the garden wall. The creature's head followed, its feelers waving in the air, hunting for prey. Finally, a gleaming black body pulled itself into view, grasping the wall with six hooked legs.

Wow! A stag beetle! Max thought, his

eyes level with the beetle's enormous jaws. There were thirty different species of stag beetle in the United States, but Max had never seen one in the wild before. Hardly daring to breathe, he crept forward for a closer look, but the insect must have spotted him. Opening the hard black casing on its back, the beetle spread its wings and whirred away into the evening sky. Max watched until it was just a tiny dot. He couldn't wait to add it to his insect records.

Max *loved* insects. He kept a notebook filled with facts about all the bugs he observed in the garden and yard. The stag beetle was his most interesting find yet.

"Max!" Mum called to him from inside

the house. "Where are you? Come and see what I got for you!"

Max's mum worked at an auction house, and sometimes she brought home unusual things that they couldn't sell. Max never knew what to expect. One time she'd brought him an old pocket watch, and once she'd even given him a suit of armour!

Max jumped up, pulling a handful of leaves off the oak tree for his pet walking sticks, and then raced back through the overgrown garden. His mum was sitting at the kitchen table. In front of her lay an old book with a battered leather cover.

"Take a look," she said with a smile.

On the front cover was a picture of a golden scorpion, its stinger raised like a dagger above its head. The title letters were a faded gold, too.

"The Complete Encyclopedia of Arthropods," Max read. "Wow! Thanks!"

"What *is* an arthropod, anyway?" Mum asked, pushing the book toward him.

"An animal with a skeleton on the outside of its body," said Max quickly. "Like insects, and spiders, and scorpions, and centipedes. And even lobsters. Where did the book come from?"

"That old mansion on the edge of town was being cleaned out," said Mum. "The book had fallen behind one of the shelves in the library. It had probably been there for years – it was covered in dust."

Max wondered who had been the last

person to read it, all those years ago. The book seemed even more special now that he knew where it came from.

"Cool!" he exclaimed, stroking the worn leather with his fingertips.

"I had a feeling you'd like it," Mum said. "No wonder, it's full of bugs!" She ruffled his spiky hair. "Take it up to your room, if you want, while I make dinner. I can see you can't wait to get your nose into it."

"Thanks, Mum." Max grinned and picked up the heavy book in both hands. He rushed out of the kitchen and upstairs.

Max's bedroom was *crawling* with bugs. Rubber spiders dangled from the ceiling, a row of plastic beetles stood on the window sill, and the walls were covered with posters of tarantulas, scorpions, dragonflies and caterpillars. The only *real* bugs, though, were Max's stick insects, which sat nearly as still as the plastic ones, almost impossible to spot inside their glass case among the twigs and leaves. Max had named them Oak, Ivy and Rose, after their favourite foods.

Max opened the top of their cage and hurriedly put the leaves in, so they could eat when they woke up at dusk. Then, barely able to contain his excitement, he took the encyclopedia to his desk and opened it. On the inside of the leather cover, there was a pocket with a magnifying glass tucked inside. *Cool*, Max thought. He started to turn the old, yellowed pages carefully. They were packed with facts about all sorts of

amazing creatures – long-necked assassin bugs, huge-bellied trapdoor spiders, giant centipedes – and there was a detailed drawing of each one. The pictures were so lifelike that the bugs looked as if they were about to crawl out of the book!

Across the two pages in the middle of the book, there was a map of a blue sea scattered with islands. Next to each island was a different picture: a tiny palm tree, a bird or an animal. Max squinted and leaned in closer to one that was marked with a black scorpion. Something was written on the island next to the scorpion's curved tail, but the letters were too small to read. Then Max remembered the magnifying glass and flicked through the pages until he reached the inside cover. He took the magnifying glass from the pocket. It was much older and heavier than the one inside the Bug Finder Kit he'd got for Christmas. The handle was wooden, worn smooth where it fitted his hand and engraved at the end was an insect head with curling feelers. Max hastily turned back to the map. Peering through the magnifying glass, he could just figure out the words next to the scorpion, written in black, curly letters.

"*Bug Island*," he whispered. "Wow. I wish I could go there. . ."

As he said the words, Max felt a strange tingling in the tips of his toes. Then the room started to swirl around him, making him dizzy. It was worse than the time he'd ridden the Death Loop roller coaster three times in a row. He squeezed his eyes shut and tried to breathe normally, but it was no use. His stomach flipped over, and for a moment he felt like he was falling. Then, as suddenly as it had started, the funny feeling stopped.

"That was weird," said Max, opening his eyes. Then he rubbed them in disbelief. He wasn't in his bedroom. He wasn't even in his house. He was sitting on damp ground, in the middle of a forest! Above him towered a tall tree with a smooth trunk. Except . . . Max frowned. The trunk was thick and bright green, with lots of thin branches sticking out of it.

What a funny tree, he thought. He looked

up to see if he could tell what kind it was from the leaves and branches, and gasped in surprise. Instead of leaves, all he could see were huge white petals, surrounding a great yellow circle. It wasn't a tree – it was a giant daisy!

Max's heart began to pound as he stood up and looked around. Beyond the gigantic flower was a real tree – the biggest he'd ever seen. Its rough bark seemed to go up and up for miles, as high and wide as a skyscraper.

"It's as if everything somehow got bigger," Max said to himself. "Or," he murmured with a gulp, "I got *smaller*. But how could that be?"

Max looked down and noticed he was still holding the magnifying glass.

As he stared at it, Max heard a strange thumping sound, like heavy footsteps. He shoved the magnifying glass into his pocket and listened hard. The footsteps were getting louder. No, not *louder*, Max realized. *Closer. . .*

The earth under Max's feet trembled slightly. Whatever was making the footsteps was *big*. Very big. And it was heading his way! Max felt a cold shiver creep down his spine. He ducked behind the giant flower. For a few seconds, the footsteps got even louder. Then they stopped.

Max held his breath and peeked around the stem. On the other side was an *enormous* creature. As Max watched, it scuttled sideways on eight jointed legs, waving a pair of huge, vicious-looking pincers.

Max gasped. It was a scorpion more than twice his size! The giant creature loomed over him, its sharp, curved stinger ready to strike!

BB

SCORPION RIDE!

Max jumped sideways as the scorpion's stinger stabbed down toward him. He gasped in horror as it crashed into the very spot he'd been standing on only seconds before.

Run! a voice in Max's head screamed. He had to get out of there before the scorpion could attack again. He knew only too well how dangerous a scorpion's venom could be. A line from his latest copy of *Bugs Weekly* magazine popped into his head.

"The first effect of the deadliest scorpion sting is intense, unbearable pain."

He raced through the blades of grass that stretched above his head, jumping over the log-like twigs that littered the forest floor and dodging fallen leaves that were bigger than he was.

"Next comes sickness and fever."

He ran in a zigzag, hoping to confuse the scorpion.

"And then, finally, death."

Max could hear the thud of the scorpion's feet on the ground as it chased him, getting closer and closer and louder and louder with every step.

The air was hot and sticky, and soon Max was out of breath. He wracked his brains, trying to remember what else his magazine had said about scorpions.

"Scorpions move very swiftly and can climb most surfaces."

So there was no point trying to escape up a tree. Not that Max was big enough to climb one of the skyscraper trees anyway. Even the gnarled roots that twisted over the surface of the forest floor rose far above his head. *But maybe I can climb* under *one of the roots and hide where the scorpion's pincers can't reach?* he thought.

Max decided it was his only chance. Summoning all his remaining energy, he raced toward a tangle of tree roots. He had almost made it, but then disaster struck. He lost his footing on the mossy ground and went flying. He scrambled up as quickly as he could, but it was too late – the scorpion was standing over him, its razor-sharp pincers snapping.

This is it, thought Max. *I'm going to be eaten alive by a giant scorpion.* He closed his eyes and waited, his heart beating against his ribs.

"What are you doing here, little lizard?" rasped a voice.

Very slowly Max opened his eyes. The scorpion was still there. It was clicking one claw open and shut, and waving the other one threateningly. Very cautiously, Max looked around to see who had spoken.

"Well?" asked the scratchy voice.

Max's mouth fell open. It was the scorpion who had spoken! For a moment he could only stare at it.

"Why are you here?" the scorpion demanded.

"I d-don't know. I don't even know where I am," stammered Max, not quite believing he was actually having a real-life conversation with a scorpion. "And I'm not a lizard, I'm a human being."

"A *what* being?" The scorpion took a couple of steps sideways.

"A *human* being," said Max.

"What's that?" The scorpion's huge jaws opened and closed as it spoke, revealing a cavernous hole of a mouth. "You don't have many legs, so you can't be one of us. And what's that stuff on your head?"

Baffled, Max put his hand up to his head. "Oh, that," he said. "It's hair."

"It's haaaaaaaair," the scorpion repeated slowly, as if hearing the word for the very first time. Its eight eyes glittered. "You're the strangest little thing I've ever seen," it said. "What am I going to do with you?"

It paused for a moment, staring at Max. Then, with a sudden lunging motion, it grasped him firmly around the middle with its pincer. Max cried out as he was lifted into the air, over the scorpion's head, and placed firmly on its back.

"Hold on tight," said the scorpion.

"What are you doing? Where are you

taking me?" Max asked, trying to sound braver than he felt.

"We're going to see Barton. He'll know what to do," the scorpion said, snapping its pincers together. Then it turned and broke into a jerky run. Its back was made of hard segments, like armour plating. Max grabbed on to the edge of one of the plates to keep from falling off. Then he glanced behind him nervously to check where the creature's stinger was. The huge bulb, with its sharp barb, curled above him. The stinger was just like a claw, curved at the end and sharp as a knife. The segments of the tail fit perfectly together, like the metal plates on the suit of armour Max's mum gave him. Max stared at it in amazement.

He was sure that no one had ever looked at a scorpion's stinger while sitting on its back before. Despite the danger, Max couldn't help feeling excited. *I'm riding on a giant, talking scorpion!* he thought in amazement.

Now that he wasn't quite so afraid of being eaten, Max had time to examine the rest of the scorpion more closely. He could see that its pincers were fat, not thin, which meant that it wasn't one of the most venomous species. Its shiny, armoured skin was as black as coal.

It must be an emperor scorpion, thought Max. Emperors were the largest type of scorpion in the world. If Max was at his normal size, the scorpion would be as big as his hand – but now that he was tiny, it seemed the size of a horse!

Max peeked out between the creature's pincers, which it held in the air as it galloped through the tall blades of grass. Bright flowers bloomed all around, and towered over them. Max could make out vast bushes with thick, leathery green leaves. Warm, damp air rushed into his face as the scorpion scrambled over a rotting branch as long and high as an eighteen-wheeler. It was like being in the coolest video game ever invented. But as they reached the other side, the scorpion stopped suddenly, nearly causing Max to go flying through its pincers.

A large creature blocked their path. Its

brown, scaly skin gleamed in the dappled sunlight. Beady eyes stared straight into Max's, and a forked tongue flicked from its mouth, tasting the air. From the folds and blotches on its skin, it didn't take Max long to figure out what it was.

An alligator lizard, he thought with a gulp. *A* huge *alligator lizard that likes to eat scorpions. And it's looking very hungry. . .*

LIZARD ATTACK!

The lizard's tongue shot from its mouth like a whip. Then, slowly, it lumbered forward. Max held his breath. It was gigantic. The ground shook with every stamp of its big, clawed feet.

"How nice of you to drop in," it hissed, "just in time for dinner."

Max gulped. From where he was sitting,

the lizard looked as big as a dinosaur. It could easily win a battle against the scorpion. As for the tiny human being on its back. . .

"Back off, you scaly bully," said the scorpion. It raised its stinger threateningly, ready to strike. The stinger's pointed tip was hanging right next to Max's head, a bead of white venom on the end. Max edged away from it, lying down as flat as he could and peering over the scorpion's eyes.

The lizard hissed. "I don't like it when my snacks fight back," it spat. It advanced again, backing the scorpion up against the branch they'd just climbed.

Max knew that the emperor scorpion was well armed. Its huge, powerful pincers and venomous stinger made it a dangerous enemy. But the lizard's scaly skin would be far too thick and tough for the scorpion's stinger to pierce.

There has to be some *way out of this*, Max thought, his heart pounding. *Maybe the scorpion can outrun it?* He looked at the lizard's powerful legs, and swallowed hard. Scorpions could run fast, but the alligator lizard looked quick, too, and it wasn't carrying a passenger.

The lizard opened its mouth, showing its sharp, pointed teeth, and suddenly leaped forward. Max clung on tightly as the scorpion scuttled to the side, dodging out of the lizard's reach.

The lizard turned slowly to face them, its yellow eyes glittering. Once again, it stepped closer. Then it stopped and tipped its head to one side.

"What do you have on your back?" it asked curiously.

Max looked up to see that the lizard was staring straight at him. The scales on its flat, crocodile-like head were all the same size, except around its nostrils, where they were smaller and darker. Suddenly, Max remembered something.

"Quick!" he whispered to the scorpion. "His scales are weaker around his nostrils! Use your pincers there!"

"Stop that whispering!" bellowed the lizard. "What sort of thing are you, anyway?"

Max glared back at the lizard. "I'm his

secret weapon!" he shouted.

And with that the scorpion darted forward, taking the reptile by surprise. Before it could react, the scorpion snapped one of its pincers on to the lizard's nose. The lizard gave a high-pitched hiss and backed away, twisting its head in pain.

"Let's go!" shouted Max.

The scorpion charged around the lizard as it retreated, holding a clawed foot to its injured snout. But Max knew they weren't out of danger yet. The lizard might still come after them. And if it did, it would be even angrier than before.

The scorpion seemed to have realized this, too, because it was running as fast as its legs could carry it. "Thanks for the

tip," it shouted back to Max.

"Any time," said Max.

"But how did you know what to do?" The scorpion sounded puzzled. "Are you *sure* you're not a lizard?"

"Yes!" Max grinned. "I don't have any scales, and I'm not cold-blooded." He shut his eyes and held on tightly as they rushed along. "I saw it on my favourite TV show – *World of Bugs* on the Nature Channel."

"On the whatery what?" asked the scorpion, sounding confused.

Max realized then that the scorpion had probably never watched TV.

"I once saw a scorpion defending itself from a lizard that way," he explained.

"It's a good idea. I never would have

thought of it," said the scorpion admiringly. "I thought we were going to be eaten for sure. I'm Spike, by the way."

"I'm Max."

"I think we lost him, Max," said Spike happily, glancing behind him. "Well, we better get back to camp ASAP. Barton will be wondering where I am."

Max held on tight as they raced through tall grass that nearly knocked him off Spike's back and they clambered over the huge leaves and twigs that covered the forest floor. After what felt like hours, Spike began to slow down. Max started to feel nervous again. Spike seemed friendly, but Max couldn't be sure. Emperor scorpions had up to thirty hungry babies at a time, which rode around on their mother's back just like he was doing on Spike's now. Perhaps Spike was taking him home for supper – and he was going to be on the menu!

"Nearly there," said Spike, making Max jump.

"Where?" Max asked.

"You'll see."

Ahead of them was a patch of bright sunlight between the trees. Max wondered if it was the edge of the forest. There was a humming sound in the air, which was getting louder as they galloped closer.

Spike scurried around an enormous, thorny bush, and suddenly they were in a large clearing. The sunlight slanted through the trees onto a wide-open space the size of a football field. Flying insects hung in the damp air, buzzing noisily. All over the ground, and on rotting tree trunks and branches, hundreds of enormous beetles, spiders, centipedes and woodlice crawled, slithered and scuttled.

Max gasped in surprise. Everywhere he looked there were giant bugs. It was as if the old encyclopedia his mum gave him had come to life!

ARMY OF BUGS

"Here we are," Spike said cheerfully, picking Max off his back and placing him on the earthy forest floor.

Max rubbed his eyes in wonder. He'd never seen so many different kinds of bugs in one place. There were insects from all over the world! As he stared, a line of army ants from South America marched past him, moving in unison. Max wasn't surprised, because he knew that army ants were always working together in the wild. They even built nests and bridges using their own bodies by holding on to one another, just like circus performers making a pyramid. Max had seen them in books and on TV, but he'd always wanted to go to South America and see them for himself.

"What's *that*?" asked one of the ants as it passed, waving its feelers in Max's direction.

The other army ants turned to look.

"Looks like a hairy worm," said one.

"Might be tasty," said another.

"Silence in the ranks!" snapped one of the bigger ants.

Max raced after Spike, who had scuttled ahead. The army ants were huge. If they decided to eat him, he wouldn't stand a chance!

The damp air was full of the buzz of bees, the whirr of wings and the whine of mosquitoes, which sounded as loud as sirens to Max's tiny ears.

Just ahead of them, the forest floor seemed to be shaking. Suddenly, with a pop, the ground exploded, and soil and sand rained down on them.

Earthquake! was Max's first thought. But before he could move, four thick, hairy black legs emerged out of a hidden tunnel in the soil. Eight black eyes glistened as four more legs and a huge, round body emerged from the burrow.

A trapdoor spider, Max realized with a gulp. *Bugs Weekly* had featured them in a venomous species special. *"Fast, aggressive, and full of deadly venom,"* it had said, *"with powerful jaws and sharp fangs, which they use to stab downward into their prey. They can also run extremely fast."*

He flung his arms over his head and shut his eyes, waiting for the spider to attack.

But instead, Max heard Spike's scratchy voice. "Hello, Webster," he said.

"H-hello, Spike," came a quiet voice, almost a whisper. "Sorry, d-did I make you jump?"

Max crept close to one of Spike's back legs and tried to make himself as small as possible. But the trapdoor spider had seen him. "W-w-w-what's *that*?" he asked, pointing a thick leg at Max. Max shrank back even farther.

"Oh, that? That's Max," Spike said, using his tail to point at him. "Don't worry, he's not a lizard. He's a human bean."

"*Being*," Max interrupted cautiously.

"What?" said Spike.

"I'm a human *being*."

"Yes, yes," said Spike, turning back to the trap-door spider. "And that stuff on the top of his head is called *hair*."

"H-hello, Max," said the spider. If he hadn't been an enormous, venomous beast, Max would have thought that he sounded shy.

"Hello, Webster," Max said. The spider bared his knife-sharp fangs. *I hope that was a smile*, Max thought.

Webster shuffled backward into his burrow so that only his eyes were visible.

"S-sorry I can't stay and chat," he said, "But Barton needs me to dig a tunnel at the front line." The door to the spider's burrow shut behind him with a thud.

Max let out a long sigh of relief.

"Come on, Barton's just up here!" Spike called, scuttling over the top of Webster's trapdoor. Max walked around it, just in case. It was so perfectly camouflaged that no one ever would have spotted it if they didn't know it was there.

"There he is," said Spike, heading

towards a rotting log.

The log was the tallest object in the clearing. On top of it, talking to a group of termites, was a huge, brown beetle with two long feelers and enormous jaws. Max couldn't help but notice the deep scar running across his wing case.

"That has to be a titan beetle," Max muttered to himself, "the biggest beetle in the whole world!"

"I need you to build a defensive wall," the beetle was telling the termites in a deep, booming voice. "A line around the edge of the clearing. That might hold those vicious lizards off for a while." The termites saluted and ran off. The beetle turned to look at Spike. When he saw Max his battle-hardened, scissorlike jaws dropped open.

"Well, well, well, Spike," he said. "What do we have here?"

"I thought it was a lizard, sir," said Spike. "But it says it's a *human being*."

Barton flicked his feelers and looked at Max closely. "A *human being*," he bellowed. "No, I've never heard of one of those before." He tapped his front feet thoughtfully. "Well, we'll worry about that later. Name?"

"Max," said Max.

"Friend or foe?"

Max thought about this for a second. "Friend," he said.

"What do you think, Spike, old buddy?" asked Barton.

"I like him," Spike declared. "He helped

me fight off a lizard. He knew just where to attack. Right on the nostril. I'll try to remember it for next time." Spike started snapping his pincers at an imaginary enemy.

"Hmmm. Useful in a tight spot. I like that in a soldier," Barton said. He scuttled down from the log and up to Max. "I'm Barton," he introduced himself. "Leader of the Battle Bugs."

"*Battle* Bugs?" Max asked curiously. He thought he knew every type of insect, but he'd never heard of Battle Bugs. "What are they?"

"We're an army, of course," Barton said, standing up very straight and flicking his feelers impressively. "An army of bugs. All the creatures you see around you now at

Bug Base Camp are under my command."

"But why do you need an army?" Max asked.

"Why?" Barton repeated. He turned to Spike. "Doesn't he know about the war?"

"I'm not sure," Spike said, raising both his pincers and clicking them together, which Max supposed was a scorpion's way of shrugging.

"The reason we need an army," Barton continued, turning back to Max, "is that we're under attack!"

Max blinked up at him, casting an eye over the browny-black scar on Barton's back. "From the lizards?"

"Yes, from the lizards!" Barton boomed. "Where do you think I got this scar from?

Have you been living inside a cocoon?"

Max thought of his bedroom, the old book and the map. "I'm not from here," he said. "I don't even know how I got here. Could you explain the lizards and the war and everything?"

Barton let out a sigh. "We'll need a map." He began drawing one in the soft earth with one of his front legs. Max recognized the shape from the map in the book – it was Bug Island. Then, Barton drew another island.

"This is Bug Island," Barton tapped the first island with one of his front feet. "And this" – he tapped the other island – "is the Reptilian Empire. The two lands are separated by a narrow stretch of sea. Or they were, until recently."

He drew a line between the two islands.

"The Reptilian Empire has a mountain on it, at the edge of the coast closest to ours," Barton continued. "But it turns out it's no ordinary mountain. A few nights ago, there was a terrible rumbling, and then fire came shooting out of the top of it!"

"It must be a volcano," Max exclaimed.

"A vol-what-o?" Spike asked.

"A volcano," Max repeated. "They're made when hot lava from deep inside the Earth bubbles up. It sounds like it erupted."

"Erupted!" Barton said.

Max nodded. "Yes, that's when the lava bubbles over the top and pours down onto the land below."

"That's exactly what happened," Barton

said, sounding impressed. "Red-hot rock came pouring down the side of the mountain and into the sea. In no time at all, the two islands had been joined together. And once the rock cooled, the lizards immediately began using it as a bridge to invade."

Max felt his heart sink. Lizards were bugs' most deadly predators. If they were invading the island, every single bug's life was in danger!

"I was there that night," Barton continued, "and had a run-in with one of the first lizards to make it on to the island. The slippery fellow caught me by surprise and cracked my wing case, damaging the wings inside."

Max gasped. "So that's where your scar comes from. Can you still fly?"

"Not at the moment, I'm afraid. My wings are still healing. But that hasn't stopped me from taking on the those scaly monsters in other ways!"

Max was impressed by Barton's bravery. "So you formed an army of bugs to fight back against them?" Max asked.

"Yes indeed," replied Barton. "But I'm sorry to say that the lizards are winning."

"You saw how strong they are," Spike said to Max. "And there are even bigger ones than that slimy monster who attacked us."

Barton nodded. "The lizards have been advancing for days. Now they almost have us surrounded. We need to come up with the perfect plan – something that will out-smart those tongue-flickers once and for all." Barton lowered his voice. "Or – and I hate to say this – we're all doomed!"

HORNET'S-EYE VIEW

"Maybe I can help," said Max.

Barton looked at Max closely. "How? If you don't mind my saying, you're, uh, kind of small."

"Do you have any claws?" Spike asked, prodding him with his pincers.

"No," Max said.

"Or a stinger hidden somewhere?"

Barton asked, circling Max and tickling him with one of his feelers. Max laughed and shook his head.

"Do you shoot acid from your bottom, like a bombardier beetle?" Spike asked, looking at Max's behind curiously.

"No!" Max laughed again. "You bugs can do amazing things that humans can't. But the one thing we do have is very big brains. Maybe I can *think* of ways you can use your special skills against the lizards."

Barton whisked his antennae back and forth like two long, black whips. "Hmm, yes, I suppose it's worth a try," he said. "What do you need to do this thinking?"

"Well, first, could I have a tour of the island?" Max suggested.

"Of course," said Barton. "And I know just the bug to take you." He wiggled his body, and a high-pitched, grating sound rang out across the clearing. Max realized that Barton was rubbing two of his body segments together to make the sound. *Another one of the amazing things bugs can do,* he thought.

A loud, droning buzz echoed around the clearing, then a dark shadow blotted out the sun. Max looked up and saw a winged shape zooming toward them. It buzzed like a noisy engine, and its wings beat so fast that a wind whipped around Max's ears.

The flying insect landed next to Barton and Spike. Its antennae, which sprouted above its big, black eyes, made it look as though it was scowling angrily. Its abdomen was striped bright orange and black, and ended in a long, pointed stinger.

A giant hornet! Max thought nervously. He wasn't usually afraid of stinging insects, but now that he was the size of a bug himself, a stinger like that would be deadly. It was almost as long as he was!

"That was very quick," said Barton approvingly.

"Yeah, well, I was close by, wasn't I? Scaring off some spies," said the hornet fiercely. "Stinkin' tree frogs! They won't be bothering us again, though," she added.

"Nice one, Buzz!" Spike said with a grin.

"Yes, well done, Buzz, old pal," said Barton. He pointed a feeler at Max. "This is Max. He's a human being."

"He's a what?" asked the hornet.

"A human being," Barton repeated. "With a very big brain."

"And hair," Spike added.

"Oh," said the hornet.

Barton turned back to Max. "Max, meet Flight Commander Buzz, the leader of our flying squadron," Barton said.

The hornet nodded her huge, orange head. Max nodded hello, too, trying not to stare at Buzz. He'd always thought that hornets had two wings, but up close he could see that Buzz actually had four. In addition to the two big eyes on the side of her face, she had three more in the middle of her forehead. *Fascinating!* Max thought.

"Max is new here," Barton told Buzz. "He says he's going to help us come up with a plan to beat those rotten lizards. But first he needs a hornet's-eye view of the island. Could you take him on a flight?"

"No problem," said Buzz.

Max looked at the hornet. "Really? Cool!"

"Hop on," said Buzz.

"Here, I'll give you a pincer," Spike offered. He grabbed Max and placed him on Buzz's back, just behind her head.

"Ready?" asked Buzz.

"Ready," said Max, his heart pounding. Buzz's back was covered in bristly hairs. Max held on to them and gripped tight with his knees.

The hornet's wings began to whirr,

making Max's body shake. This was going to be a bumpy ride! Buzz stretched out her wings, and they rose into the air, straight up like a helicopter.

"Report back soon, soldiers," Barton commanded, waving goodbye with his feelers. "Be careful. I can't afford to lose either of you to the enemy."

"Don't you worry, sir, those slimy reptiles will never catch me!" Buzz shouted over the whirring of her wings.

"See you later!" Spike called, snapping his pincers in the air.

Buzz swooped off, rising until they were up among the trees. Max could see the whole clearing below them. They were so high that Barton, Spike and all the other bugs looked like tiny dots.

Once he got used to the buzzing and the whirring of Buzz's wings behind him, Max was actually very comfortable among the hairs on Buzz's back, and he started to enjoy the hornet's skilful flying. They zigzagged between the tree trunks, zooming up and down, narrowly missing branches and dangling vines. Holding on tight, Max carefully looked down. The forest floor was so far below him, it made his head spin. This wasn't like flying in an aeroplane, or even being on a roller coaster. There was no seatbelt to keep him from falling off – and the ground was a long way down. . .

Just as Max was starting to feel dizzy, the forest ended and they were suddenly

flying over a beautiful beach. It was very bright after the greenish light of the forest, and a sparkling blue sea lapped against the sand below them.

"There's the bridge!" called Buzz, shouting above the hum of her wings.

Max took a deep breath and leaned over Buzz's side again. Down below, a rocky path formed a bridge to a nearby island, just as Barton had said.

The Reptilian Empire, Max thought with a shudder. It wasn't covered in lush forest like Bug Island; it looked more like a desert, with rocks as grey as thunder clouds and the occasional shrivelled-up shrub here and there. Max looked back at the bridge, and started in shock. The bridge appeared to be moving! But as Buzz dived lower, Max realized that it wasn't the bridge that was moving, it was a stream of reptiles *on* the bridge, all making their way to Bug Island.

"There's more and more of 'em every day," Buzz shouted grimly.

It seemed like every type of reptile and amphibian imaginable was crossing the bridge. There were geckos, chameleons, snakes, frogs and toads, all slithering, creeping and hopping forward. The huge, scaly creatures moved their heads from left to right, their flickering tongues tasting the air. They were looking for bugs, Max realized, shuddering. There were enough to eat every creature on Bug Island.

Buzz turned and followed the stream of reptiles along the beach. To Max's horror, he saw that they were heading into the forest further up the coast. If they were entering the forest, then surely it wouldn't be long before they arrived at the clearing where Barton and the bug army were camped!

"We're doing our best to stop 'em, but there's just too many," Buzz called to Max, swooping over a sandy hollow where some tarantula spiders were fighting a group of green lizards. Max held his breath as one of the tarantulas reared up on to its back legs and hissed. A lizard whipped its tongue out angrily. The tarantula fought back by flicking its legs back and forth until the air around it became thick with a cloud of hairs.

Max let out an excited gasp. He had read about tarantula hair-flicking, but never thought he would actually get to see it. He knew from his books that hairs released from the tarantula's legs would stick to its prey and cause a painful rash or even temporary blindness. He watched as the lizard shrieked and stumbled on the sand.

"Go, tarantula!" Max shouted.

As they flew on, Max spotted a praying mantis standing upright and fanning its wings. He knew from his books that this was what the mantis did when it was under attack. Max looked closer and saw a gecko darting back and forth across the sand, taunting the mantis. Max wished there was something he could do to help, but now that he was small, the gecko was the size of an alligator. Buzz was right – there were too many reptiles, and they were too big and strong.

Buzz slowed down to hover above a large grey rock. Squatting on top of it was the biggest, ugliest lizard Max had ever seen. It had dark brown scales, and its beady black eyes glinted with evil. It turned its huge, mud-coloured head from side to side as it surveyed the marching creatures, and its yellow forked tongue darted in and out.

"Keep in line!" it hissed at a group of

small frogs. "Or I'll come down there and flatten you!"

"That's General Komodo!" shouted Buzz, zooming lower. "The commander of the lizard army!"

But before Max could reply, the huge lizard turned its head upward, its beady eyes flashing with rage. Then, as quick as a cracking whip, its long, sticky tongue flashed out, heading straight for them!

BB

LIZARDS CLOSE IN

"Look out!" Max cried as the giant lizard's tongue flicked through the air.

Max was almost thrown off Buzz's back as the hornet swerved to the side. He clung tight to Buzz's hairs, his legs dangling in mid-air as the hornet shot upward, just out of reach of the enormous lizard. As they swooped away over the army of deadly reptiles, Max felt his hands starting to slip. He couldn't hold on any more. "Help!" he cried.

But it was too late. Max lost his grip, and suddenly he was falling through the air. He squeezed his eyes shut as the ground raced towards him. There was no way he could survive a fall from such a great height. Any second now, he would smash into the ground and . . .

Thump!

His heart pounding, Max opened his eyes. He was sitting on a huge green leaf as big as his mum's bed. Max couldn't believe his luck – if he'd slipped a second later, he would have missed the leaf completely.

But just as he was starting to relax, a sharp breeze came whistling through the forest. The leaf swayed and dipped and immediately became a huge green slide.

"Help!" Max called as he started slipping down the shiny surface. "I'm falling!"

"Hold on!" he heard Buzz call from somewhere above.

"I can't! There's nothing to hold on to!"

Max picked up speed. The air rushed past his face, causing his eyes to water. He saw the edge of the leaf getting closer, and the forest floor stretched out below, crawling with deadly lizards.

"Help!" Max cried again. He was slipping and sliding and falling and—

Suddenly he was rising, being yanked up into the air by the back of his T-shirt.

Max craned his neck and saw that Buzz

had somehow managed to hook one of her front legs under his shirt collar. Buzz swooped back in towards the tree and plunked Max down on to a huge branch.

"Sorry, pal," Buzz said, landing next to him. "I thought you were a goner for a minute."

Max took a couple of deep breaths. He'd thought he was a goner, too. It was a pretty scary existence being the size of a bug. Once his heart had stopped pounding so hard, he peered down over the edge of the branch. The forest floor was far below him. He could just make out the brown shape of General Komodo, still sitting on his rock. The branch swayed slightly in the breeze. Max felt sick.

"Thanks, Buzz," he said faintly.

"Come on, hop back on," Buzz said. "We'd better get back to Barton."

Max clambered up one of Buzz's hairy legs and back into position behind her head. The hornet's wings whirred into flight again.

Buzz headed up towards the treetops. Max's heart was still racing, but he made himself look down toward the forest floor. It was swarming with reptiles and amphibians, and it wouldn't be long before they reached Barton's camp. He had to come up with a plan – the bugs' lives depended on it. They were almost back at Base Camp when something caught his eye, sparkling in the sunlight.

"What's that over there?" Max yelled to Buzz.

"Pollen River," Buzz replied. "It flows down from the Fang Mountains."

"Can we take a closer look?" Max asked.

"No problem!"

Buzz flew over the clearing and towards the river. As they got lower, the air was filled with the roar of rushing water. Max held on extra tight and leaned over to take a look. Down below, the river frothed and bubbled like a witch's cauldron. On the far side, the ground sloped up toward a row of jagged mountains shaped like pointed teeth. Max could see why they were called the Fang Mountains. Nestled below the mountains, the far riverbank was covered with a blanket of wild flowers, in the middle of which stood a young tree. Max looked back at the gushing water.

"Do you think the lizards would be able to cross the river?" Max asked Buzz, thoughtfully.

"Nah, the water moves way too fast for them," Buzz replied.

Max smiled. The bugs might not be able to *fight* the lizards, but perhaps there was a way to escape from them.

"I've got an idea!" Max cried. "Let's get back to Barton."

"Sure," said Buzz. Putting on a burst of speed, the hornet zoomed back to the clearing and landed on the rotten log next to Barton and Spike.

"Welcome back, soldiers," said Barton.

"Good to see you," said Spike with a wave of his pincers.

"What is the enemy's position now?" Barton asked.

"Closer than ever, I'm afraid, sir," Buzz told him. "But the tarantula squad is fighting well."

Barton nodded. "Good old tarantulas," he said. "I knew they wouldn't let us down."

"I have an idea for a plan," Max said excitedly.

Barton spun around to look at him. "Go on," he said.

"Pollen River," Max said.

Barton looked at him blankly.

"The lizards can't cross the river," Max

explained. "The water's too fast for them. But maybe we can."

Barton nodded. "Those of us with wings can. But what about the ones who can't fly? Or can't fly *at the moment*. We can't leave them stranded – that would be breaking the Battle Bug motto."

"What motto?" Max asked.

"Never leave a bug behind," Barton, Spike and Buzz all cried in unison.

Max frowned. "There must be some way to get everyone across," he said. "If only we had a boat."

"A what?" Barton barked.

"Something that floats," Max replied.

"Leaves float," Spike suggested.

"Yes," said Barton. "But we need something that can take our whole army across – like a bridge."

Just then a line of ants marched past.

"That's it!" Max shouted. "The army ants! They could form a bridge for the other bugs to cross."

"A bridge of army ants could never hold me," Spike said gloomily. "I'd just squish them."

"Yes," said Barton. "They'd never be able to hold the bigger bugs."

Max wracked his brains. He thought back to the river. It wasn't even that wide. If only he could think of some way for them to get across. If he were his normal size, he'd probably be able to leap across. He thought of the stream in his grandparents' woods, and how his grandfather had bridged it with a log. A log. From a tree.

"The tree!" Max cried. "We'll make a bridge from the tree on the other side of the river. That way we only need to get Barton across first."

Barton, Spike and Buzz all stared at him blankly.

"There's a little tree on the other side of the river, right next to the water," Max explained. He turned to Barton. "Titan beetles like you are great at chomping through wood. Even though you can't fly at the moment, if we can get you across first with the army ants, it could still work. You could chop the tree down so it falls across the river, and it would make a bridge strong enough for all of us to use!"

Barton, Spike and Buzz looked at one another.

"Well, I suppose it *might* work," said Barton. "And I'm certainly the bug for the job. I'll have you know I once munched my way right through an oak tree!"

"While you're gnawing the tree, I could start airlifting bugs across, sir," said Buzz, flying into the air and circling around their heads. "The other winged insects could help, too."

"Excellent. We have a plan. Action stations, everyone," commanded Barton. "Well done, Max. Your very big brain has come in very handy."

Max grinned, but his smile soon faded

as a worried-looking centipede scurried toward them, all its legs rippling as it ran.

"Sir!" it cried, "The lizards have reached the trail to the clearing. They're almost here!"

BB

AMAZING ANTS

"What are we going to do?" Spike cried.

"We need to get everyone's attention," Max said, looking around at the scuttling, buzzing bugs filling the clearing.

Quick as a flash, Barton wriggled his huge brown body, making a screech so loud that Max had to put his fingers in his ears. It was a horrible sound, like someone scraping their fingernails down a blackboard, but it worked. Everyone turned to see where the noise was coming from.

Once they were all quiet, Barton spoke. "This is Max. He's something called a human being and he has a plan."

"And a very big brain," Spike added.

Hundreds of insect eyes stared at Max.

"We think we've found a way to escape from the lizards," Max shouted.

There was a humming and buzzing sound from the bugs as they all started talking excitedly.

"Silence!" Barton bellowed. "There is no time to lose. General Komodo and his army of tongue-flickers will be upon us at any moment. Army ants! Assemble at the front."

The army ants all marched forwards. Max gasped. There were so many of them!

Barton quickly explained Max's plan. When he finished, the captain of the army ants stepped forwards.

"Permission to speak, sir?" she said. Barton nodded. "Our bridges are made for other ants to walk across, not beetles. It could break."

"Yes," said Barton. "I thought of that. Just make the bridge as strong as you can. I'll have to take the risk."

Max stared at the brave bug. He hadn't thought about how dangerous his plan would be for Barton. If the bridge broke, the Battle Bug commander and the ants would all be washed downstream and drown. But if they didn't try, *all* the bugs would be eaten by the lizard army.

"All right, we've got to get to the river," Barton finished. "All flying bugs, follow Buzz. Take a passenger if you can. The rest of you, come with us!"

"Good luck!" Buzz called, taking off with a family of woodlice on her back. A couple of bees followed her with several tiny beetles clinging to their legs.

"I-I suppose we'd better go, too," a voice behind Max whispered. He turned to see Webster the trapdoor spider coming out of his burrow. "D-do you want a lift?" he offered shyly. "Eight legs are faster than two."

Max nodded, and clambered onto the spider's hairy back. Barton, Webster and

Spike led the way, and behind them scurried the entire Battle Bug army.

It didn't take long to reach the river. The water covered them in spray as it tore past them.

"There's the tree," Max called to Barton. "Do you think you'll be able to gnaw through it?"

Barton looked at the young tree swaying in the breeze. "Absolutely!" he declared. "It's nothing but a mid-morning snack! Ready, ants?"

"Positions, everyone!" shouted the army ant captain. "We can use the rock in the middle of the stream. Build from here to the rock, then from the other side of the rock to the tree."

Max held his breath and watched as the ants began, using their bodies as building blocks. Two of them grabbed hold of each other with their legs and huge jaws. Another ant grasped hold of them, then another. Soon there was a huge, linked line of them on the pebbles beside the stream.

"Start building into the water," commanded the captain.

A group of ants shuffled to the edge of the stream and stood firmly, anchoring the group to the side. Others clambered over them and began building out on to the fast-moving water. More ants joined them, and then more. Soon the bridge was at least twelve ants wide and five thick. Gradually, the bridge grew until it reached the rock.

More ants scrambled across the bridge, over the rock, and began building the second phase of the bridge. Soon the army-ant bridge stretched right across to the tree on the other side of the water.

"We're ready, sir," the captain told Barton as she took her own place on the bridge.

"Excellent work, captain," Barton replied. Then he signalled to Buzz, who landed nearby. "If anything happens to me, Flight Commander," he said seriously, "the Battle Bugs are yours to lead."

"Yes, sir. I won't let you down," Buzz said gravely.

Max clenched his hands into tight fists as Barton took a first careful step on to the bridge. He knew that ants were very strong insects, and that each one could carry many times her own weight. Barton was bigger than twenty of them put together, however, and they were already struggling against the raging current. If just one ant let go, the whole bridge would collapse and Barton would drown. As the first four of his legs stepped on to the bridge, Max could see the ants' bodies straining, holding on to each other even more firmly. Next to Max, Webster had dug a burrow and was peeking out. Buzz flew in nervous circles overhead.

As quickly as he could, Barton scurried forwards. With every step, the bridge trembled and shook dangerously.

"Ouch!" cried one of the ants.

"Hold steady!" shouted another.

As Barton struggled on to the rock in the middle of the stream, one of his back feet knocked an ant into the rushing water. The other ants cried out and the bridge wobbled, but it didn't break.

"Help!" the ant yelled as the water started to sweep her away.

Thinking quickly, Barton reached out towards the ant with his long feelers.

"Grab on!" he shouted.

The ant stretched her legs up – but she was just out of reach.

"Come on, soldier! You can do it!" Barton shouted.

The ant made another grab and just managed to catch the very end of one of

Barton's feelers. Slowly, Barton pulled her through the water until she could climb on to the rock.

"Thank you, sir," the damp ant gasped, her knees knocking.

Barton nodded. "Never leave a bug behind," he said firmly. "Now wait here, soldier. I have a job to do."

With that, he climbed over the rock and down the other side toward the second half of the ant bridge. He placed his first pair of legs carefully, but just as he was about to put his second pair on the bridge, his front foot slipped and he slid sideways into the stream. All the bugs gasped.

"Barton!" Max cried out, rushing forwards.

The brave beetle was holding the rock with two legs, while the rest of him was in the water.

"We've got to help!" Max gasped.

"I'll fly you over," said Buzz. "Quickly!"

Max grabbed one of the hornet's legs, and Buzz rose into the air.

"Hang on, Barton!" Max called as he dropped from Buzz's leg on to the rock.

Barton was clinging to the rock with his front legs, but the stream was flowing too fast for him to haul himself back to safety. Max grabbed one of Barton's legs and pulled with all his might, while Buzz hovered overhead and tugged on Barton's feelers. With a great heave, Max fell over backwards and Barton finally struggled back on to the rock.

Barton shook himself, scattering water all over Max.

"Thank you," he said gratefully.

"Never leave a bug behind!" Max and Buzz chorused.

"Let's try again," Barton said. "Ready, ants?"

"Yes!" the ants called out. For the second time, Barton stepped off the rock. Max held his breath, but this time Barton didn't stumble as he slowly made his way across. Finally, all six of his feet touched the pebbles on the other side. He'd made it!

A cheer of shrill ant voices echoed across the stream. Buzz gave a sigh of relief and wiped a leg across her forehead. Max jumped up on her back, and she flew over to where Webster was hiding.

"You can come out now!" Max smiled. "Barton's safe."

Barton was already working on the tree, his powerful jaws cutting into the tough bark. The ants started breaking down the bridge, scuttling over each other one by one until they all reached the other side and were lined up in neat rows next to Barton.

Barton looked up as they got closer, but didn't stop chomping. He was already halfway through, and the tree was bending over the stream. Finally, it gave a loud crack.

"Stand back!" shouted Max as the sapling snapped. It landed with a crash on the shore, making a sturdy bridge across the river.

The bugs cheered, and Max grinned in relief. His plan had worked!

"Good work, Barton!" shouted Max.

Barton scurried on to the bridge, waving his feelers.

"Advance, troops!" he shouted. "There's no time to lose!"

Max and Webster stood aside as the first of the bugs – woodlice, earwigs and some of the smaller spiders – swarmed across. Max noticed that the team of tarantulas, some of them wounded and limping on seven legs, had joined the back of the line.

"Enemy advancing! Enemy advancing!"

Max turned to see Spike scuttling

towards them at full speed.

"The lizards are here," he yelled. "They're right behind us!"

Max turned towards the forest, and his stomach lurched. Crashing through the trees was a line of huge lizards, with General Komodo in the lead!

BB

BUGS FIGHT BACK

Max gulped. There wasn't enough time to get all the bugs across the bridge before the lizards arrived. Their only option was to fight.

"We have to hold them off while the others escape," Max said firmly. Rushing over to a bush covered in long, sharp spines, he broke one off and waved it in the air like a sword.

"Come on, Spike," he shouted. "Let's show those scaly thugs what we're made of."

Spike grinned. "OK, Max!" he said. "Jump on!"

Max ran and leaped on to Spike's back.

"Scorpion squad!" Spike cried, turning toward the bugs. "Come with me!"

Several scorpions scuttled forward. Max recognized fat-tails, deathstalkers and bark scorpions, all of them with deadly venom in their stingers.

The squad got into position, forming a line between the bridge and the lizards, with Spike and Max at the front. It was like being at the head of an army of knights, everyone waiting, ready to attack. Max could feel the ground trembling as hundreds of reptile and amphibian feet stomped toward them.

"Halt!" boomed the deep, rumbling voice of General Komodo. The lizards stopped and stood facing the scorpions, their scales gleaming in the sun.

"It's all over, you pathetic bugs," General Komodo roared, his long tongue flicking from his mouth as he spoke. "You're all going to be eaten – you might as well give up!"

"No chance, you overgrown tadpole," shouted Spike. "Come here and get us – if you dare!"

General Komodo let out a growl so loud it caused Max's rib cage to vibrate. "We're going to be eating you bugs for breakfast, lunch and dinner," he spat. "And I think I'll start with *you*" – he pointed a claw at Spike – "and that ugly *thing* on your back."

Max waved the spine in the air. "You'll have to *beat* us first!" he yelled.

Spike and the other scorpions cheered, and the lizards hissed. Spike raised his pincers and his stinger to make himself look as threatening as possible.

"Use your pincers and your stingers," Max whispered to the other scorpions. "Go for the nostrils – that's where they're weakest."

"This is your last chance!" cried General Komodo. "Surrender now! Or prepare to die a painful death."

"Never!" replied Spike. "Go back to your own island, tongue-flicker!"

"That's it!" shouted Komodo. "Charge!"

The line of lizards surged forwards, their teeth bared and their long claws glinting.

"Charge!" shouted Max and Spike together, as Spike rushed forwards.

Max almost fell off Spike's back as they smashed into the first lizard. Spike aimed his stinger straight for its nose. The reptile fell back, writhing on the ground in pain.

As Spike prepared to face another lizard, Max felt something splatter all over his back. He turned and saw a salamander with its tongue fully extended, sticky mucus dripping from the tip.

"Look out, Spike!" shouted Max.

Spike turned just in time. His deadly stinger rushed through the air over Max's head and slammed into the salamander's skin. The salamander reeled its tongue in with a hiss and limped away. Max breathed a huge sigh of relief and looked around at the other scorpions. They were fighting just as bravely as Spike. Soon, almost all the enemies were falling back, yelping in pain.

Max looked back towards the bridge. Only a few insects remained on their side of the water. "The other bugs have nearly made it," he told Spike. "If we retreat now, we should be able to get across the bridge before the lizards have time to follow us."

"But I'm just starting to enjoy myself!" Spike joked.

"What's the matter with you, you useless reptiles!" shouted General Komodo to his troops. "Squash them! Destroy them! EAT them!" His huge feet pounded the earth as he came crashing forwards.

"On second thought, maybe it is time to go," said Spike.

"Scorpions!" shouted Max. "To the river!"

All the scorpions turned and raced back to the bridge. One by one, they scuttled quickly across. Spike and Max climbed on after them, but to Max's horror, the lizards were closing in.

"Run, Spike! Run!" Max shouted, clinging tightly to Spike's back. They were only halfway across, and already the first lizards had reached the bridge.

General Komodo yelled more commands. "After them!" he screeched. "Move, you lazy lizards!"

Spike rushed even faster towards the other bugs, who were gathered anxiously on the far bank. He was almost there when one of his feet slipped, and he lurched towards the fast-moving water. Max gasped as he was sent flying forward. He clutched on to Spike with all his might as Spike dangled from the tree bridge, hanging by just one pincer. Below them the water frothed and foamed, and behind them the lizards hissed and cackled.

Then suddenly all their laughter was drowned out by a familiar droning noise from above. Buzz!

"Flying squadron, dive-bomb, now!" Buzz yelled.

Max clung on and watched as the giant hornet and other flying insects started dive-bombing the lizards on the bridge, flying at them and stinging them wherever they could. The lizards hissed and swatted at the flying bugs with their claws and tongues, but Buzz and her friends were too fast, and flew from side to side, always just out of reach.

"Hold on," Buzz yelled as she swooped in below Spike and helped nudge him back on to the bridge.

Max sighed in relief as Spike's feet touched the tree trunk. Spike scuttled across the rest of the bridge, and finally they were back on dry land.

"We did it!" Barton cried. "All the bugs have made it across."

"Yeah, but it looks like all the reptiles will make it across, too, sir," Buzz called down from where she was hovering above them all.

Max looked back across the river and saw more and more reptiles and amphibians slithering on to the tree trunk. "Quick," he shouted. "We have to destroy the bridge!"

Crowding around the edge of the bridge, the bugs pushed with all their might. But the lizards were making it too heavy.

"Heave!" shouted Barton.

"P-perhaps I can help?" Webster scurried out from beneath the trapdoor where he had been hiding. Rushing up to the bridge, he put his front four legs against the wood and pushed hard with the full weight of his huge body. The lizards hissed in alarm as the sapling started to shake.

"Go, Webster!" Max shouted, as the bridge started to move. With one last strong push, Webster shoved the end of the bridge into the river. The lizards tumbled into the water and were swept downstream.

On the other side, General Komodo howled with rage.

"After them!" he screeched, raising a huge, clawed foot and pushing a gecko into the river. But the current was too strong, and the gecko was carried away.

"Useless creatures!" yelled Komodo. He

looked at the other reptiles and shook his head. Then he looked back across the river. "You'll pay for this, bug-brains," he snarled. "Don't think you're safe. My lizard army will find a way to get to you, and then we won't stop until we've eaten every last one of you! Especially *you*!" he snarled, looking straight at Max.

BB

FANG MOUNTAIN

The bugs let out a wild cheer as the lizards turned and slunk back into the forest. The tarantulas picked Webster up and danced along the riverbank with him, and the scorpions crowded around Spike.

"Save the celebrations for later, soldiers!" Barton shouted over the noise. "Let's get to safety first."

Buzz zoomed overhead. "I'm going to find out where those lizards are headed while there's still some light," she said.

"Good idea." Barton nodded. "We'll make camp farther up the mountain. The fireflies will light up to show you where we are."

Buzz zoomed off, and the other bugs trudged happily up the mountain to find a place to camp for the night. Soon they found a sheltered spot at the foot of a cliff, and Barton gave the order to stop. All the bugs began making themselves as comfortable as they could. Webster dug a burrow, the woodlice and earwigs found stones to crawl under, and the spiders spun their webs. As Max watched them, he thought of his own bed back home. Now that all the excitement was over, he couldn't help wondering if he would ever find his way back to his own world.

A faint hum in the sky became louder and louder, and Buzz landed next to Max. Barton, Spike and Webster hurried over.

"What's the news, Flight Commander?" Barton asked.

"The enemy has retreated into the forest, sir," replied Buzz. "But I sneaked up on their camp to listen in on their plans. Tomorrow, General Komodo is going to send them out looking for another place to cross the river."

"Just as I thought," Barton said, rubbing his feelers together. "This battle is won, but the war isn't over." He climbed on to a log and called for attention with a shrill noise. Everyone fell silent and turned to face him. "Soldiers, you have all battled admirably today, but there's one bug – or I should say *creature* – that deserves our special thanks." He pointed one of his feelers at Max. "We would all be lizard food right now if not for Max and his brilliant plan!"

"And his very large brain!" Spike added.

All the bugs whooped and chirped and buzzed. Max felt his face growing hot. He looked around at the cheering beetles and the crickets rubbing their wings together enthusiastically. Some of the woodlice had curled themselves into balls and were rolling around on the ground in excitement.

Max grinned. It had been incredible being on Bug Island, and getting to meet such amazing creatures, but what if he never got home? His smile faded as he thought of his mum calling him for dinner and discovering that he had disappeared.

"What's up, Max?" Spike asked, placing a pincer on Max's shoulder.

"I'm just a little worried about how I'll get back to my own world – the human world," Max explained.

"Well, how did you get here?" Buzz asked.

"I don't really know," Max replied. "So I don't have a clue how I'll get back." He started feeling slightly sick.

"Do you have to go?" Barton asked. "We need all the help we can get. The lizards might be defeated for now, but they'll be back."

Max nodded. "I have to get home. My mum will be worried about me. But once I figure out how I got here, I promise I'll be back."

"Come on, bugs," Spike said. "Max helped us; now it's our turn to help him!"

"True, true," said Barton. "We need to help you remember how you got here."

"What was the last thing you did before you came to Bug Island?" Buzz asked.

Max thought. The last thing he could remember was looking down at the map through the magnifying glass. The map was in his bedroom, a world away, but the magnifying glass was still in his pocket.

He took it out and turned it over in his hands.

"I looked through this, and then I sort of fell through it and found myself here."

"Well, maybe if you look through it again you'll fall back?" Spike suggested.

"That's a good idea!" Max said. He took a deep breath and looked down through the magnifying glass. But nothing happened.

"Oh, dear," said Spike.

"Are you sure you looked down?" Buzz asked.

Max nodded sadly. "Yes, I was looking at a map of Bug Island, and the next thing I knew I was actually here."

"Hmm," said Barton. "Puzzling."

"I-I have an idea," Webster whispered.

"What is it?" Max asked anxiously.

"W-well, if you looked down to get here, then m-maybe you have to look up to get back." Webster sighed and retreated back toward his trapdoor.

"It's worth a try," said Barton.

"OK," Max replied. With one last look around the clearing full of bugs, Max held the magnifying glass up to the dark sky. As he looked through the glass he felt a strange tingling in his feet. "I think it's working," he cried.

"Goodbye, Max!" chorused his friends.

"Goodbye!" Max called.

"Come back soon!" Spike added.

Max continued looking up through the magnifying glass. For a moment, all he could see was a clear dark sky, but then it was hidden by a swirling black fog. Max's stomach lurched as he felt himself being pulled up and up . . . until he landed with a gentle bump.

Max blinked. He was back in his bedroom, holding his magnifying glass, looking at the map of Bug Island in his new encyclopedia.

"Max!" came his mum's voice from downstairs. "For the last time, dinner's ready!" she shouted impatiently.

Max looked at the spider-shaped clock above his desk. Hardly any time had passed at all, but he'd been on Bug Island for hours. He'd talked to insects, ridden a scorpion and fought a battle against huge hungry lizards, but here it was still dinner time!

At least Mum hasn't been worried, he thought.

"Coming, Mum!" he called.

Max put down the magnifying glass and looked at the map of Bug Island again. Down there somewhere were Spike, Barton, Webster, Buzz and all the other bugs, in the middle of a war. Would he ever see any of them again? He hoped so. Just as he began to close the book, something caught Max's eye. He opened the page again and peered at the map. It was hard to see the islands without the magnifying glass, but he was *sure* the black scorpion had waved a pincer at him.

Max stared at the page for a moment, then grinned. He closed the encyclopedia and carefully placed it on one end of his bookshelf, next to a centipede-shaped bookend. He traced the picture of the golden scorpion on the book's spine.

He had a feeling he'd be back on Bug Island very soon.

REAL LIFE BATTLE BUGS!

Titan Beetle

As one of the world's biggest beetles, the titan truly lives up to its name. An adult specimen can grow to be a huge six-and-a-half inches long! They boast a strong, flat body with long legs, large antennae and a seriously impressive pair of short, sharp mandibles to ward off predators. (Its jaws are so strong they can even snap a pencil in two!)

The beetles spend most of their lives underground, with only the adult males venturing out to find a female. They can be very hard to find. They are attracted to light, however, which scientists use to their advantage – that's if they dare to get close to those fearsome mandibles!

Ants

Ants are one of the most highly successful and widespread insects in the world. They're found on nearly every landmass on Earth and evolved over 110 million years ago – back when dinosaurs ruled the planet!

One of the most fascinating ways ants

work together is when they build bridges – with their own bodies! Ants are tiny creatures, so even the smallest gaps between high branches or shallow streams can seem impossible to cross. But by linking their legs together, ants can form bridges to where they need to go.

If that isn't amazing enough, the fire ant can even build an entire life raft out of all the workers in their colonies. That way they can survive flood waters and float safely down rivers!

For more bug facts, fun downloads, competitions and to discover all the books in the Battle Bugs series visit **battlebugs.co.uk**

WIN A FAMILY PASS TO PAULTONS PARK!

To celebrate the epic Battle Bugs series we've got a family pass to Paultons Park, home of the new mini-land Critter Creek, to give away! The lucky winner will also receive a set of six Battle Bugs books, so your family can have a bug-filled day together. Start off by heading to Critter Creek at Paultons Park and exploring the mixed-up critters at Critter Creek, before snuggling up at bedtime and reading the books together.

Visit www.paultonspark.co.uk/competitions/battlebugs to enter the free competition before it closes at midnight on 31st December 2015.

Good luck!

BACK TO BUG ISLAND!

General Komodo and his army are on the attack. Komodo has assembled a fleet of fearsome horned lizards for a mountain assault. The Battle Bugs have to come up with an airtight plan – or risk losing everything.

Max's return to Bug Island is dangerous – but the Battle Bugs need his help!

1

Press the scorpion out of the card.

2

Start by folding the lines that form the head.

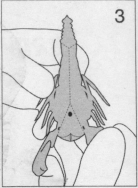

3

Fold along the scorpions back and the base of the tail to give the overall shape.

4

Fold the lines through the middle of the scorpion to form a zigzap shape.

5

Fold the middle back in on itself and firmly fold down the back again. Then fold the lines in the tail to give it a curve.

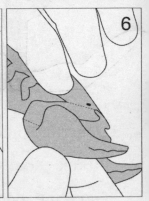

6

Finally, fold the two lines in each of the arms.